Tommy's First Day of Kindergarten

Tommy's First Day of Kindergarten

A. Matthew Huff

Copyright © 2025 James M. McCracken

JK Press
Redmond, Oregon

All rights reserved.

ISBN: 979-8-9986565-9-0

This is a work of fiction. Names, characters, places and incidents are either the product of the author's imagination or are used fictitiously, and any resemblance to any actual persons, living or dead, events, or locales is entirely coincidental.

To my parents

John & Kathleen Huff.

"Good morning, it's time to wake up," Tommy's mom said.

Tommy jumped out of bed. He was excited because today was his first day of kindergarten.

All summer long his parents had helped him to learn his address and telephone number. They had also walked to school with him so he would know the way.

Tommy took a bath, brushed his hair,

and put on his new clothes.

"I'm ready for school," he said.

"Not so fast," his mom said. "You have to eat your breakfast first."

After breakfast, Tommy's mom walked with him to the school. "Now, pay attention, Tommy, so you won't get lost."

Nour
Labrov
Secachouds
Canalet!
dours

As they stood outside the classroom door, Tommy's mom gave him a kiss on the cheek.

"Now, remember. When school is over, wait for me here. I'll come and walk home with you."

Tommy met his teacher.

He made a new friend.

He painted, played at recess,

and had a snack of milk and cookies.

When it was time to go home, the children lined up. The teacher had them all say their ABCs before she opened the door.

Tommy forgot his mom's instructions to wait for her. He followed as the teacher led the children outside to the parking lot and the waiting parents. But when Tommy didn't see his mom, he slipped around the side of the building without his teacher noticing and began to walk home.

Down the street he walked,

looking back at the school.

Once he could no longer see

the school, he became afraid.

He rubbed his eyes and cried,

but he kept walking.

At the end of the block, he remembered what his mom and dad said. "When you come to the end of the block, look both ways before crossing the street."

When he reached the end of the next
block, he turned the corner.
To his surprise, he saw his mom!
She was pushing the stroller with his
baby brother inside. Beside her, he
saw his little sister holding her dolly.

Tommy ran into his mother's arms and cried with relief.

"You were supposed to wait for me at school," his mother said.

"I forgot," Tommy said.

"It's important for you to remember," she said.

"I will next time," Tommy said.

"You're safe, now," his mother said.

"Let's go home."

On their way, Tommy told his mom

about all the fun he had at school

and how he couldn't wait to go there

again.

The End.

www.ingramcontent.com/pod-product-compliance
Lightning Source LLC
Chambersburg PA
CBHW041201100726
47911CB00016B/815